George C. Wellner

The medical graduate and his needs

George C. Wellner

The medical graduate and his needs

ISBN/EAN: 9783742828767

Manufactured in Europe, USA, Canada, Australia, Japa

Cover: Foto ©Andreas Hilbeck / pixelio.de

Manufactured and distributed by brebook publishing software
(www.brebook.com)

George C. Wellner

The medical graduate and his needs

THE

MEDICAL GRADUATE

AND

HIS NEEDS.

BY

GEORGE C. WELLNER, M. D.

DETROIT, MICH.:
GEORGE S. DAVIS.
1894.

CONTENTS.

PREFACE.

The following production, although small in compass, is the result of a good deal of observation and reflection.

It is now years ago that the author first observed that, in common with all young physicians on their entrance into practice, he constantly encountered certain difficulties respecting which neither his *Alma Mater* nor the books had taught him anything. However, these difficulties were not owing to a positive want of professional acquirements, but wholly to an unqualifiedness to use them to the best advantage. With a view to self-improvement he began to note down, as occasion in his own practice and that of others suggested, specifically all such of the more important and elementary difficulties as appeared to him not to have sufficiently attracted attention, adding, at the same time, such hints, cautions, and specific directions as his judgment suggested. The fruit of this labor is this little volume. Its being the only one of the kind, may serve as its *raison d'être*. The customary challenge, "Why do ye spend money and time for that which is not bread?" does not apply to it.

Although designed chiefly for students and young practitioners, it can be read with profit by "children of a larger growth."

ON THE STUDY OF MEDICINE.

If it is a truth of study in general that inborn aptitude is a fundamental prerequisite to success, it is a
truth of the study of medicine in particular. He who
presumes to tread the tedious and distant path leading
to the temple of Esculapius without this aptitude,
without a decided natural bent for it, will succumb too
soon to the burden of his task. The elasticity of the
mind, so essential to the attainment of the goal, will
give way, impatience, discontent and fatigue will set
in, and the career entered upon with no special calling
for it, is abandoned, or the study will at best be continued with indifference and irksomeness, without a
prospect of success or reward whatever. But not only
the mental, the physical powers as well must be ade-
quate to the exertions required by the study of medicine. How many a young man whose health does not
possess the requisite ruggedness to bear the strain
without detriment, has snatched away from him
through premature disease or death the reward of
years of successful labor, before the aim of which has
been reached, or soon after when the already shattered
health is altogether undermined by the hardships of
active professional life! Really, how often do the
best founded hopes and the most justified expectations

come to premature disappointment and sad grief! And how urgent is it to address the voice of warning to those who are about to engage in the study of medicine without this important coadjuvant, good health! On the other hand, he who does not command the means to prosecute extensively, or with at least approximate thoroughness, so spacious, so important a subject in its results, as medicine, ought, as in bounden duty, to abstain from its study. For he would fail to acquire that degree of scientific education and professional drill which is so immediately essential to establish the success of practice, to secure the respect of the public, and to beget that self-confidence which is so indispensable to the physician. Only he who has by means of a liberal education and extended medical and other studies laid a secure foundation, can with any certainty hope to attain to success, maintain his independence, and consider the future as secured. How painfully frequent is it to see physicians, who, having lacked the pecuniary means of thoroughly studying their profession, never succeed in issuing from the sphere of indigence, remaining ever in a subordinate position, engaged in a continuous struggle for existence, vexed by cares for the future! And is there possibly a sadder lot than that of a conscientious medical man, who, in a calling full of privations and hardships, can not earn even the means of satisfying the demands of a modest livelihood, and when adverse circumstances encroach upon him cannot dispense with even the charity of others?

His extremely arduous studies over, the young physician enters upon practice. Now can it be said that practice affords him any recreation or respite from the exertions he has just escaped? By no means. For to the ordinary fatigues of practice, there are added the irregularities of living and the emotional perturbations which no conscientious, no true physician can shun, can shake off. So far as bodily exertion, wear and tear of body, is concerned, it may confidently be asserted that that involved in the practice of medicine exceeds that of any other profession. There do indeed obtain in the profession diverse degrees of exertion according to the position of the practitioner; thus, while the exertions required of the physician in the larger towns are generally fairly tolerable, those peculiar to country practice amount to actual toil, and are frequently insufferable. Take medical practice at its best. The eminent practitioner of the metropolis, as well as he of a more comfortable practice, whose patients in point of intelligence, influence, and pay, leave little or nothing to be desired, who makes his professional rounds by carriage, aided by numberless other advantages, even he finds practice fatiguing enough at all times. How much more downright toilsome and exhausting, then, must be the practice of that large class of physicians in cities and the larger towns, who, as beginners, or what is still worse, practitioners of advanced age—but too often the case —are compelled to walk their visits which many times extend to distant parts of the town, and up many a stairway in lofty tenements? If to this are added the heat of summer, the rigor of winter, the other inclemencies of weather, the frequent necessity of visiting patients late in the evening, the disturbance of sleep, the irregular hours for food and sleep, and other necessities, the deprivation of many other comforts of life, the numerous occasions for agitation, the numberless exquisite vexations, it must unqualifiedly be conceded that the practice of medicine is harder, more burdensome, more exhausting, than that of any other profession. And yet these hardships and privations appear well-nigh insignificant compared with those of the country practitioner, he of that heroic class, "the toiling many, and the resting few." In all seasons, in all states of weather, day or night, afoot or in a lumber wagon, over bad roads, and through deep sloughs, he is in fact the unique of professional men. Let him who has no experience of the hardships of such practice, make an effort at a conception of them. Let him conceive the physician as being roused at midnight from a sound sleep and a warm bed, to go into the country a dozen or more miles. The roads are bad, the night is dark, and, as a consequence, following the right road difficult, to say the least. After several hours' ride of much discomfort, due to broken sleep, the raw air or rain, the uncertainties as to the right road or direction, the apprehensions of upsetting the vehicle, if not to the more serious possibilities of winter, he arrives at the house of his patient. As a rule no comforts await him here, and if, having rendered his services, the condition of the roads, darkness, or the nature of the patient's case is such as not to compel him to tarry all night, he has a right to improve the opportunity for self-congratulation. But if detention should be his lot, perhaps as often the case as not, his time will then for the remainder of the night belong in a large measure to the patient, sleep will probably not visit him, and one thing or another will yet have to be suggested capable of whiling away the tedium and bore of those hours.

To these multiplied exertions are added the disadvantages to health accruing from changes of temperature and inclemencies of weather, unavoidable influences made operative in the highest degree by the increased susceptibility of the body to them in the night and early morning hours. Taken all in all, the daily and nightly hardships of practice cannot fail to impress themselves upon the health of the physician however hardy he may be. The young practitioner whose health is all but fortified by a strong constitution, whose body is in nowise inured to the severe privations of practice, will find but too soon that these exposures of the very opposite kind are most prolific of various constitutional disorders, more especially of nervous prostration and catarrhal and other inflammatory affections of the air-passages, etc. His health once permanently impaired, his fondest hopes and best aspirations together with years of conscientious and successful labor are blasted. He can no longer hope to attain anything like success in his profession; and, what is perhaps more serious and afflictive, his years, the exhaustion of his means, and above all his impaired health, render success even outside of the profession highly improbable. On the other hand, the veteran practitioner whose constitution has more successfully withstood the buffets of practice, at last falls a prey to rheumatism or "poor health," and he must remain content if he is only occasionally vexed, his body only incommoded at intervals; if practice is not made difficult or altogether impossible, and some grave form of heart- or other disease does not set in to burden and embitter the last years of life.

These are some of the considerations which the candidate of medicine ought well to weigh in mind at the very outset of his medical studies. Good health, inborn aptitude, and, as a rule, ample pecuniary means, these are the conditions of success. With them, all the added and superadded obstacles and difficulties of medical practice will prove to be comparatively trivial, or so many "sufferings devinely appointed as joys;" without them the result will at best be average professional ability, that is, a wretched mediocrity which is everywhere at a notorious discount.　Average ability in the physician in the present overcrowding of the ranks of the profession means mediocrity of success,and mediocrity of success means humiliation, debt, poverty—*poverty* that will ride him more oppressively,more persistently, than did the Old Man of the Sea bestride Sinbad:

> " Misplaced in life,
> I know not what I could have been, but feel
> I am not what I should be."

METHODIC CLINICAL INQUIRY.

Method is defined by Coleridge, in his admirable essay, to be " a progressive transition from one step to another." "Without method," says this great thinker, " all things in us and about us are a chaos, and so long as the mind is entirely passive—so long as there is an habitual submission of the understanding to mere events and images as such, without any attempt to classify and arrange them, so long the chaos must continue. There may be transition, but there can not be progress; there may be sensation, but there can not be thought; for the total absence of method renders thinking impracticable, as we find that partial defects of method render thinking a trouble and fatigue; but as soon as the mind becomes accustomed to contemplate not things only, but likewise relations of things, there is immediate need of some path or way of transit from one to the other of the things related—there must be some law of agreement, of contrast, between them—there must be some mode of comparison; in short, there must be method. We may, therefore, assert that the relations of things form the prime objects, or, so to speak, the materials of method; and that the contemplation of these relations is the indispensable condition of thinking methodically.

Of these relations of things we distinguish two principal kinds. One of them is the relation by which we understand that a thing must be; the other, that by which we merely perceive that it is. The one we call the relation of law, using that word in its highest and original sense—namely, that of laying down a rule to which the subjects of the law must necessarily conform; the other we call the relation of theory."

To a successful examination, method is indispensable. It gives perspective to the beginner, and comprehensiveness to indifferent and mediocre talents; it leads the sanguine to sobriety, and it is the measure which guides the judicious and experienced. To discard all methodical procedure would entail circumlocutions, iterations, and omissions; but more especially does an examination, devoid of method, lack the band which unites the symptoms and groups of symptoms, the examiner having in the most favorable case an aggregate of phenomena with which he is unable to cope otherwise than by wasting his strength and time upon them individually. Though it is not always practicable to adhere to a stereotyped order of examination, and one must often occupy himself with what the patient chooses to bring forward, yet in the mind, at least, one must hold to some order, and, when there obtains no longer any contraindicating circumstance, return practically to it. There are, it is true, highly-gifted diagnosticians, whose perspicuity and great comprehensive grasp of

mind may dispense with much that is superfluous;
but the only test of the correctness of their diagnoses is a mental review of a methodic examination.

Nothing in lieu of experience is, therefore, of
more importance to the success of the young clinician than method.   No other means will so well enable him to turn to profitable account his attainments,
skill, and mental acumen; certainly, the want of no
other means is capable of causing him so much disappointment and abatement of professional dignity.
The failures of the young physician, let it be remembered, are owing less to a want of positive acquirements and experience, than to inexpertness, unqualifiedness to use them.   It is not so much in point of
fact, the presence of the medical attributes—the
open eye, the quick ear, the lively touch, the keen
smell, etc.,—as the ability to use them well, that
conditions success. If the young physician will but
consider the source of all his embarrassments, uncertainties, and disconcertions at the bedside; his doubt
and vacillation in diagnosis; his irresolution, impatient
expectation, and shifting in treatment,—he will find,
upon mental introspection, not a want of thought or
matter for thought, but a want of order; he will find
that there is transition, but no progress; that there is
sensation, but no relativity of thought.

There are two methods essentially adapted to the
needs of the clinical beginner, namely, the Synthetic
and the Analytic.   There are still other methods, but

each and all of them are too complex or difficult to be practical, and the junior diagnostician cannot hope to use them with any degree of facility whatever. Neither is any one, nor all of them together, more scientific, more comprehensive or more reliable than the synthetic or the analytic—the synthetic reversed. It is true, expert diagnosticians, men of great experience and close observation, gradually acquire what has been defined as non-communicable intuition and tact; a kind of natural method which permits them to dispense in a measure with a more rigorous application of the synthetic or analytic. But, on the other hand, the great bulk of practitioners of nearly every denomination, and, with a few exceptions, of nearly all grades of ability, those who carp at the study of method, as well as those who appear only practically indifferent to it, all, observe in a manner and measure, though perhaps unconsciously and instinctively, the one or the other, as the case may be, of these two methods.

The Synthetic, Genetic, or Historic Method, is divisible into four serial parts: 1. Medical Genealogy; 2. Medical Biography; 3. History of the Existing Affection; 4. Present Condition of the Patient.

1. Medical Genealogy investigates the health and the diseases of lineal and collateral antecedents, and relatives of several generations. It sets out with the parents, adverts, if necessary, to brothers and sisters, grandparents, etc. Rigorously employed, medi-

cal genealogy must not omit or slight age, habits, occupation, standing, inclination, idiosyncrasy, etc.

2.   Medical Biography begins with the birth of the individual, passes in detailed review the epochs, affections ·and phases of evolution of early life, and arrives through the histories respective of health and disease, at the present constitution, diathesis, cachexia, and existing affection and its remote and its more proximate causes.

3.   History of the Existing Affection opens with the investigation of the circumstances under which the disease originated, elicits its etiological or causal moments, acquaints itself with its inception, its course, and the treatment hitherto pursued.   It must segregate every important fact relative to social position, occupation, predisposition, habits, idiosyncrasy, etc. Like the preceding parts, it must give its result historically serial,

4.   Present Condition of the Patient follows the same order, inasmuch, as the present morbid phenomena taken collectively precede in the order of examination the individual synergies, etc.   .

In its most comprehensive and rigorous application, this method must not pass over any organ or function, and from the sum total of the product, differential diagnostics separates the pathological from the spurious phenomena, and combines them with the medical genealogy, medical biography, and history of the existing affection; then comparing, relating, and arranging them, sets them to a pathological likeness to which comparative diagnostics assigns its proper nosological position.

The synthetic is the more accurate and comprehensive method. It is true it leads with difficulty, but then with certainty to a knowledge of complicated and wearisome maladies, which from modification and change by time and therapeutic interference have lost their marked character and the order of their expression. It is admirably adapted to the making of case-records, and as a corrigent and sheet-anchor when the physician finds himself misled through other methods, or is unable to arrive at any satisfactory issue.

Against this method may be urged that it occupies much time, implies great labor, sweeps up much useless material, and that the examination of the present condition in physiological order is fatiguing to the patient.

The synthetic method is purely interdicted when the disease is of a very painful nature, where the patient is much exhausted, and when there is otherwise danger in protracting the examination. It is partly inadmissable in young children, deaf-mutes, disorders of the mind, or where the statements are for any reason unreliable.

The Analytic, or Retrospective Method, is the opposite of the synthetic. It commences with the inquiry into the present condition of the patient, and endeavors to ascertain the prominent changes of structure and the phenomena subordinate thereto. The result of this inquiry is taken as a starting point for conducting either the history of the existing affection or the medical biography, and, if need be, the medical genealogy. The synthetic method views the disease as developing, and genetically unfolds the case with the aid of the phenomena it historically elicits. The analytic, on the other hand, regards at outset the disease as already a collective whole, as already developed, at least for diagnostic and therapeutic purposes. It begins with the present condition of the patient, by seizing upon the principal or most proximate phenomenon, resolves it into its component parts, assigns it its diagnostic relation, and, passing on to other single and aggregate phenomena, it extends retrogressively, not necessarily over the entire present condition of the patient, history of the existing affection, medical biography, and medical genealogy, but only to those moments which directly or indirectly relate to the disease. This method, unlike the synthetic, need not in the end, owing to the greater objectivity of its moments, make a comparative estimate of the value of the respective symptoms, but directly betakes itself to the general principles of diagnostics to determine their character by comparing them with similar or identical pathological likenesses.

The analytic method is chosen where there is

danger in a protracted examination; where a simple ailment obtains, and where the patient must be spared. Though these circumstances afford a pretext and opportunity for slighting and ignoring the less proximate but, therefore, not any the less important phenomena, and for giving the simple manifestation of the disease a favorite interpretation. This method, though far shorter and more convenient than the synthetic, presupposes greater praxis and critical judgment in the physician which enable him to make a diagnosis from the few given data only.

Though one can indicate the idea that should determine the direction and course of an orderly and well-connected examination; and, moreover, approximatively indicate how to ask, or examine, but *what* the physician shall ask, his experience, education and genius can only suggest. For this reason all quiz-formulæ or tables are useless, and even objectionable, for the physician of mediocre ability will but too much incline to admeasure every disease to his limited formula, and to omit necessary questions not contained in it.

The tact, the nice perception, the ready power of appreciating and doing what is required by circumstances, with which the physician conducts himself at the bedside; the order and precision of his questions; the exhaustive catechisation and the skillfully conducted exploration; the observance of a proper firmness as well as a ready forbearance at the right time

and place; the avoidance of unessential, time-con-
suming examinations; the elicitation and development
of every essential moment; and the arrangement of
the result to form a just adaptation of parts to each
other, a connected whole, of which the probability and
necessity of the connection can be proved, according
to anatomical and physiological laws, these are the
criteria of a methodic examination and of a capable
diagnostician.

ON THE PHYSICIAN.

"1. Medicine is, of all the arts, the most noble, but owing to the ignorance of those who practice it, and of those who inconsiderately form a judgment of them, it is at present far behind all the other arts. Their mistake appears to me to arise principally from this, that in the cities there is no punishment connected with the practice of medicine (and with it alone), except disgrace, and that does not hurt those who are familiar with it. Such persons are like the figures which are introduced in tragedies, for as they have the shape and dress and personal appearance of an actor, but are not actors, so also physicians are many in title, but few in reality.

"2. Whoever is to acquire a competent knowledge of medicine, ought to be possessed of the following advantages: Natural disposition, instruction, a favorable position for the study, early tuition, love of labor, leisure. First of all, a natural talent is required, for where Nature opposes, everything else is vain; but when Nature leads the way to what is most excellent, instruction in the art takes place, which the student must try to appropriate to himself by reflection, becoming an early pupil in a place well adapted for instruction. He must also bring to the task a love of labor and perseverance, so that the instruction taking root, may bring forth proper and abundant fruits.

"3. Instruction in medicine is like the culture of the products of the earth. For a natural disposition, is, as it were, the soil; the tenets of our teacher are, as it were, the seed; instruction in youth is like the planting of the seed in the ground at the proper season; the place where the instruction is communicated is like the food imparted to vegetables by the atmosphere; diligent study is like the cultivation of the fields, and it is time which imparts strength to all things, and brings them to maturity.

"4. Having brought all these requisites to the study of medicine, and having acquired a true knowledge of it, we shall thus, in traveling through the cities, be esteemed physicians, not only in name, but in reality. But inexperience is a bad treasure, and a bad fund to those who possess it, whether in opinion or reality, being devoid of self-reliance and contentedness, and nurse both of timidity and audacity: for timidity betrays a want of power, and audacity a want of skill. There are, indeed, two things, knowledge and opinion, of which the one makes its possessor really to know; the other to be ignorant.

"5. Those things which are sacred are to be imparted only to sacred persons, and it is not lawful to impart them to the profane until they have been initiated in the mysteries of the science."—Hippocratic Law.

In addition to the Hippocratic requisites for a physician, there are others no less important. Of importance to the success of the physician, is his own good health, physical and mental. The physician ought not to be ailing, at least not in a degree derogating on the one hand from his critical acumen, and on the other from his bodily endurance. He should not be splenetic nor petulant, least of all himself plaintive; for the solicitude for his own condition will absorb that for his patient, and thus disappoint his expectations. He should neither be indolent nor abstracted,lest many seeming insignificancies escape him.

The junior practitioner should not let a want of confidence paralyze his beginning; nor too great a presumption of knowledge dispel insurmountable difficulties. He should not be possessed of enthusiasm or trepidation for anything. In the exercise of his calling, he should be serene and earnest, firm and benign, but in every instance sympathizing. In short, he ought to appear at the bedside, in the character of the calm, deliberate diagnostician. It is no very easy matter to cast off love and hate, joy and sorrow, enthusiasm and despondency, as though they were but the mere vestures which screen our humanity; but let him not approach the bedside until he is in the clear with himself.

At the bedside the physician should avoid too cheer-ful a frame of mind which views everything on the sunny side; likewise too disconsolate a mood which pictures everything as inevitable and calamatous. The diagnostician ought so to discipline his mental and physical infirmities, that he may at the decisive moment subjugate them, and leave unhampered all his powers. The defects and faults of the patient can in a measure be amended by the examiner, but those of the latter can hardly be remedied.

The young physician should not repose his merits or demerits, as is too often done, either in the estimation of the patient or in the judgment of the public. And, to escape the numerous and exquisite humiliations by which the first years of his professional life will be checkered, he should neither allow his ambition to be cried up by fashion and a momentary success, nor to be cried down by unmerited censure. The public, the mass as such, is ever disposed to reason about physicians like a reasonless animal; and one can daily make the observation that the greatest ignoramuses, whom even luck does not favor, can maintain themselves for decades as celebrated practitioners.

Of importance to success is his deportment in the presence of the patient. For example, to enter the sickroom precipitately, cast aside hat and cane, bustle into a chair, and question hastily, is by no means adapted to lead the patient to repose entire confidence in the physician. Believing to see in the hurried examination, the discharge of an onerous duty, the patient regards his case as slighted or as already given up; to proceed in the opposite extreme, would no less defeat expectation. He who indeterminedly approaches the bedside, questions in an unsteady manner, pondering for minutes at a time after each answer, provokes impatience and awakens distrust.

The look with which one meets that of the patient is of consequence. The severe, penetrating look of the critical diagnostician overawes the timid and susceptible, and is shunned by them; while the knowing and intelligent mistrust the inordinately lax mien of the phlegmatic dullard or that of the obsequious simperer. Though the physician will endeavor, as in a measure he must, to suit his individuality to that of his patient, yet he should not place himself on a level with him. The physician, in his relation to the patient, is emphatically above alike the high and the low; he ought not to be trivial with the one, nor make concessions sacrificial of professional stability to the other. He that allows those of "quality" to make difficult his duty for him, is served right if their treatment of him is that of body-servant instead of medical advisor.

Though the physician should ever be impressive of the dignity of his calling, and, therefor, conservative of his deportment before his patient, as well as of his address to him, yet he must suit them to the exacting wants of the case. Patients are dull, dejected, sulky, fretful and querulous, and, as a matter of course, the manner of approaching them successfully must be

varied with the prevailing exigency.   But he should
forbear to act the medical histrion, who, trespassing
all bounds, sobs with the sentimental, jests with the
sportive, and sighs with the weary.   Lastly, he should
advisedly refrain from ever introducing himself to the
patient by that derisive duad popularily considered so
significant and exhaustive of medical diagnostics: a
look at the tongue and a feel of the pulse; or by that
absurd and hackneyed phrase: "Are you sick?" or
"What ails you?" etc., than which there is nothing
better adapted to fret the patient and dispossess him
of confidence in the physician.

Among the many trying situations in the early
practice of the young physician, there are perhaps few
more embarrassing, certainly none more frequent, than
that of excessive self-consciousness at the bedside.
Alive to the correctness of his every action, anxious
to conduct the examination aright, and more than ap-
prehensive of making a bad impression, he not infrequently believes himself, or rather his professional competence, to be the subject of critical observation, if not
of suspicion, by the intelligent patient and his attendants.   Fearful of prejudices and their consequences,
and as yet unfamiliar with so anxious a scene as that of
the sickroom, his mind is frequently overstimulated, a
condition of want of confidence, or better, of excessive self-consciousness, in which he can no longer
with reliable precision follow system or purpose
hatever, and where the result will at best be a par-

tial diagnosis. The anxious look and distressed countenance of the patient watchfully turned upon him;
the expectant attitude of friends and attendants
throughout the entire examination; their critical attention, whispers, and probable distrust of him, abash
him—strike him with a humbling sense of inferiority,
and he is no longer capable of examining relevantly
to the issue; he is entirely preoccupied by *how* he
questions and *how* he examines. Questions no longer
suggest themselves in orderly relation, and he asks
them as they happen to occur to him: now he queries
of bowels, now of antecedents, and now of diet, age,
etc.; questions not readily enough presenting themselves, he makes a confused pause, and next, under
the impulse of keeping busy, he abstractedly feels of
the pulse, looks at the tongue, and gives directions, to
recur again to bowels, antecedents, etc. His voice,
too, becomes indetermined, his very eye and cheek
becoming accessories, as signs, to his extreme dis-
comfiture. To escape so disagreeable an ordeal, the
clinical beginner should, before entering upon his
duty, first of all somewhat disedge his diffidence and
the novelty of the situation, by a little unreserved
converse with the attendants. But if his want of self-
possession does not with safety permit this, nor even
distinctness or coherency of speech—by no means in-
frequent when the *salon*-untutored clinical novice is
suddenly honored with a professional call to a patient
of "quality"—then let him, the first flutter attendant

on entering the house having subsided, immediately seize the only opportunity to compose himself for the examination.   Nothing is so well calculated to do this than the statement of the attendants which leaves him merely a listener.   Unless his presence of mind have returned, he should from time to time interrupt the examination to communicate the result.   He will find this much more practicable than to reserve the entire communication for the last, when the burden of speech has become great, and the anxiety of friends and attendants painfully inquisitive.

The young practitioner needs especially to be plied with motives for circumspection on the subject of misdiagnosis.   To misdiagnosticate a disease well-known to the laity, is to hazard an ultimate exposure of the mistake, the result of either ignorance or inadvertance, and its consequent odium which, not unlike that celebrated ghost, will not *down*, except at the price of his professional reputation.   Though this is in a measure unavoidable, yet it may be so minimized in the catalogue of clinical embarrassments as to be scarcely appreciable.   The young clinician coming in charge of a case that he is unable to diagnosticate can not too forcibly nor too often be preadmonished not to be precipitate in either christening the disease or in shaping its treatment.   There is, except in certain exigent cases, no occasion or press for haste whatever, and if the physician will but reserve his first-born opinion, and consider that the writing of a prescription then and there is not, as is so generally practiced, the grand prerequisite for the case; and that while still fresh in the confidence of his patrons, a little special preoccupation with the case, an hour or so spent in most thoroughly quizzing patient and attendants,—he will come to no other conclusion more often than that second thoughts are as a rule more reliable than first thoughts. Whatever mode of procedure he may, however, elect, let him in no instance, drift so far astern of duty and medical common sense, as to prescribe from mere force of habit. This abominable practice has already made the profession the butt of numberless dirisive and sarcastic reflections.

There is in all medicine no aid to practice, the acquisition of which is so ardently coveted by the young graduate as a short cut to diagnosis. To scrimp the science and the art of diagnosis to a mere effort at taw and pushpin, and to clutter his memory with the signs and symptoms of disease, appears to be the only engrossing and foodful task of the average medical beginner. And thus it is that in the first years of his practice he can neither diagnosticate nor differentiate a large number of diseases. Let him, for illustration, give on the spur of the moment the differential diagnosis of waxy-liver and cancer of the liver, parenchymatous nephritis and interstitial nephritis, mitral direct murmur and mitral systolic murmur, meningitis and myelitis, spinal congestion and spinal irritation, simple meningitis and tubercular meningitis,

and of numerous others, and he will at once discover
the result of his most exertive efforts to be at best but
so many macaronic compounds, and that there is no
compendious method whatever to diagnosis.   Let him
confront a case taken at random, say a true congestion
of the liver, and his sciolous semeiology will instantly
discover itself.   He will indeed hit upon a few of its
signs and symptoms, such, perchance, as enlargement
of the organ, pain, jaundice, indigestion, obstructed
circulation, but, then, these are common to many
other diseases of the liver, and fancy, not facts, will
finally have to complete the diagnosis.   Such diagnosticating is, to use an apt figure, like attempting to spell
a word without knowing for certain its orthography.
The medical abecedarian is, indeed, most frequently
in the predicament of the poor speller who, though
perfectly cognizant of the identity of some of the let-
ters of two or more similarly spelled words, cannot at
the price of his salvation, spell or point out certain
differences between them.   In such plight, the diagnostician need not give himself up to any soothing
hopes of bridging over his diagnostic deficits by trick,
knack, juggle, or any facile legerdemain.   Sciolism in
medicine, as in other domains of knowledge, is super-
able only by effort, hard continuous effort, effort,
moreover, in the right direction.   Let the candidate
for the degree of Doctor of Medicine relinquish his
nutshell literature of "Essentials," "Synopses," "Epi-
tomies," "Vade Mecums," "Compends," etc., let him

apply himself to the great text-books of practical medicine, pathology, hygiene, microscopy, etc., in short, let him understand, as he ought, his business, and he will unconsciously have relegated his diagnostic wool-gathering and clinical geeing and hawing and possessed himself of the coveted and only true short cut to diagnosis.

There is one branch of the medical art the practice of which is, in view of its necessity and consequence, far too neglected by the medical beginner, namely, the art of writing prescriptions. Hence the inability of many a young practitioner to write his prescriptions with indifference as to the presence of others. It matters little however capable he may be, a certain amount of embarrassment peculiar to most persons unaccustomed to show their penmanship before others, will surely possess him. This, moreover, is not a little hightened by his consciousness of the popular vulgar fancy, inborn, as it were, with most persons, especially the ignorant and half-educated, which admires nothing so much, not even orthography and grammar, as high-flourished, cursive penmanship, than which nothing is so generally regarded a more respectable mark of ripe scholarship. Painfully conscious of this before lookers on, and therefor necessarily unsteady and inattentive to the substance of his prescription, the young doctor allows himself to be hurried into writing fast, being entirely preoccupied with *how* he writes. As a result of these off-

hand exertions it not infrequently follows that after
leaving his patient he mentally comes to himself, and
then will have nothing of more pressing moment to
do than to speed after the prescription-bearer to the
apothecary's to correct some "irregularity" of dose,
etc.   To avoid such unprofitable and vexatious
experience   he   has   one   more   reason   for   hold-
ing   attendants   to   their   business,   and   for
not   tolerating   curious   folk   in   the   sickroom.
The subject may appear trifling, but it is anything but
that.   When it is reflected upon that a prescription
must first be reasoned out, then correctly, carefully
written down; that the beginner is in need at the bedside of nothing so much as self-possession; that he
would by all means avoid being seen to dwell with
long and anxious attention upon the prescription,
to write it out, as it were, by laborious installments,
advice can assuredly not be thought superfluous or
overcarking.   If prescriptions were, as they ought to
be, indited, *composed*,—and not dashed off in a moment's time with merely an off-hand mental effort, those
abominable, execrable specimens of to-day would have
an end, and accidents without number, from this source,
as well.   Let the young prescriber hearken to counsel,
and take sufficient time clearly to think out, and
correctly and legibly to write out his prescriptions.

One   more   point   concerning   tact.   The   young
physician should accustom himself to the use of the
stethoscope, as there remains no longer an excuse for

burrowing the side of one's face in the chest of the patient and thus, auscultation, circumscribe it. Multiplied as have been the arguments trumped up for immediate auscultation, enough have not yet been adduced for proof sufficient to give it warrant. It is objectionable alike from considerations of convenience, cleanliness and propriety. In auscultation of the female chest, common decency, if nothing more, demands the employment of mediate or stethoscopic auscultation.

Though the physician should keep abreast of the age in which he lives, which, for one thing, means that he ought to have at hand all the more necessary and practical appliances and instruments required for the successful prosecution of his profession, yet it does not follow from this that he should keep a very mechanic's shop. We are living in an age of instruments and appliances, where every physician is also an inventor, and where there are twenty and more instruments of a kind; and it behooves the medical beginner to be wary. Let him beware of buying instruments that will become antiquated in his possession and rusty from the wear of time before he has occasion to use them. Though his means allow him to purchase whatever of instruments and appliances he may wish, let him not have a different instrument for every other case, which is the counterpart of having a different medicine for every other disease, and prognos-

tic of quackery and medical dandyism. Let him
wisely imitate the skillful artisan who makes one instrument serve many purposes. Thus a small number of judiciously selected instruments may be put to
the greatest variety of uses, and the want of a special
instrument not be felt.

It has come from a thoughtful source that we are
fast getting to be a profession of mere mechanics, ar-
tificers; that we are dealing with our patients through
media; that we are losing certain natural powers possessed in a higher degree by our ancestors; that our
senses are becoming obtunded from want of training;
that we are neglecting the study of a most important factor in our art, viz., human nature; that it is
the cultivation of the study of human nature, more
than anything else that gives medical chicanery and
charlatanry its success and peculiar prestige.

These charges are not without suggestiveness.
For example, despite of every mark of appreciation
of the importance of the sense aids, the beginner is
to be cautioned not to neglect his sense of touch because of the employment of the thermometer. The
same may be predicated of the other senses. As to
the study of human nature, the beginner may have
learned something of temperament, but of *faith* as a
therapeutic coadjuvant he has learned nothing appre-
hensible.   Faith is the assent of the mind to anything,
but in medicine it is practically assent to whatever
the physician does or says, whether right or wrong,

true or untrue.   But it is more the *manner* than the matter that creates faith.   Thus the physician may successfully treat a case, yet not possess the patient's faith; or he may fail time and again in the same family, yet be still the idol, the incomparable.   These are pointed facts too little heeded and not at all studied. If it were more the matter, the purely scientific physician would incomparably be the most popular.   The secret of begetting faith is, the utmost self-assurance in every   act   and word,   of   which   the conscious   power   of   ability,   the   halo   of   almightiness surrounding the presence of the master-minds of the profession, is the best illustration.

ON DIAGNOSIS.

"When a patient presents himself for examination or for treatment, he tells us of certain things that he feels or sees, which are wrong, and which we call 'symptoms;' we ask him questions, and learn additional facts of a similar class; we observe him, and notice other facts which he can neither feel nor know by independent means, and these we call 'signs,' or 'objective symptoms.' From what we are informed, and from what we observe, we pass on to the inference of other facts: we believe, when some three, or four, or more changes from the healthy state are present, that other alterations exist; and this belief is more or less strong, and its character more or less definite, according to the state of medical science, and our knowledge of it, at the time the patient presents himself. We *infer* certain things, certain conditions which we cannot see, but which we may, in some measure classify, and, therefore, call by distinctive names. Thus heat of the skin is a symptom from which we infer a number of ulterior conditions. This is what we call 'diagnosis' in its practical sense."

The diagnosis begins with the inspection of the patient, and his physiognomy will first engage the attention of the physician. It is an invaluable gauge of his condition; an unfailing record of every pain as well as of every ease. Indeed, its daily and hourly suggestiveness is so marked that it is distinctively stamped even upon the faces of the attendants, and reflected from them, and that in a degree enabl'ng the observing physician unerringly to read the countenance of his patient by proxy ere he has yet entered the room. The first impression from the patient will serve to limit the inquiries of the physician to a class of diseases. Thus he will necessarily know whether the disease in hand is of childhood, old age or the parturient state; and, most often, whether of the vascular or nervous system, acute or chronic, etc. Next, the physician should assure himself of the favorableness of the surroundings for his purposes. Not infrequently it happens that on the entrance of the physician the entire household, filled with curiosity and expectation of the things to come, crowd into the sick-room; and, each eager to add his mite to the general fund of information, they wax disputatious, and sorely distress the patient The physician will do well to insist on these folk retiring ere they have yet involved the patient in a wrangle of crimination and recrimination.

The physician should on entering the sickroom note, though as unobserved as possible, everything that might be of aid to his diagnosis. A number of objects may present themselves for this purpose; ob-

jects indicative of occupation, pastime, habits, etc.
He will at a glance survey the location and condition
of the room and its contents; know whether it is
cleanly or uncleanly; whether the surroundings, persons and objects, are pleasant or unpleasant. He
will remark with especial heed the presence or absence of medical apparatus, remnants of medicines,
etc., which have been put aside or hidden, but not
sufficiently to conceal them from the discerning eye of
the sagacious diagnostician.

With many persons a scene of hurried activity and
confusion, to produce orderly arrangement, ensues on
the entrance of the physician. Let him well observe
everything transpiring in the stir around him. If he
have his senses on the alert, he will often gather many
a diagnostic datum from this, for more reasons objectionable than desirable, state of things. Thus from
misplaced and ill-timed propriety, his nose will often
be greeted by a deft attendant hurrying by him with
what is not infrequently his most valuable diagnostic
material, namely, the excrements of the patient.

It does not always happen that the patient is found
in a posture or light favorable for one's purpose, but
the physician should in no instance, unless the case
demands it, permit so vexatious a circumstance as a
dark' room or any other disadvantageous state of
things to lessen the integrity of his examination or
diagnosis.

Having inspected his patient, and exchanged such

civilities as are proper and practicable with him, the physician will request him to deliver himself of everything pertaining to his illness. The physician should listen attentively, for nothing gratifies the patient more, unless it be talk to no purpose, in which case he will cleverly lead him back and limit him to the narration of facts. During the statement, the physician has leisure to acquaint himself with the patient's individuality, culture, manner of speech, and to remark every important suggestion offered by his case: condition of the sensorium, rationality, voice, position of body and limbs, design or anxiety to ignore or slight certain circumstances or constantly to recur to them; repeated feeling of parts, laying on of hands, etc.

Having given a careful hearing to the patient's detail, the physician enters upon cross-examination. His questions to the patient should be admeasured to his understanding, yet accurate, positive and to the point; and, if the answers are pertinent, should be followed by such as arise directly or such as are taken from method. Where, owing to limited intelligence or suffering, the patient is unable to say more than "yes" or "no," the answer should be contained in the question. However, all suggestive questions should be avoided as much as possible, as many patients incline to affirm every presumption.

Such questions only as are relative to the issue should be put. A departure from this rule is admis-

sable only where the state of the mind or the disposition of the patient is such as demands advertant
circumlocution. In purely subjective symptoms, of
the actual existence of which there is a doubt, the
question should again be put, but in a different order,
with the design of circumventing either the misrepre-
sentations or answers indifferently made with the
intention of ridding himself of what is to him a
bother.

Suspension or intermission in the examination is to
be made only when the condition of the patient demands it, otherwise it would lead the physician from
his adopted course, and, moreover, give the patient
leisure to introduce matter foreign to the issue. In
violent paroxysms, the examinations should be staid,
to be resumed at the next intermission.

Every utterance of the patient is not to be credited
with veracity, though he may often underrate his ailment; in both cases, exploration should be the medium.
If any of the answers have escaped his memory, the
physician should repeat the question, though in a
manner that seems to aim at double assurance; for ab- ·
straction and absentmindedness in the physician, the
sick never excuse.

Those who, from a paucity of ideas and words, are
unable to express themselves, must be encouraged and
assisted. Such patients are, for instance, incapable of
saying anything more specific than "I feel sick " or
" I feel sick here," indicating the affected part by lay-

ing on the hand, and utterly fail to convey more definite ideas without the coöperation of the physician. But let him, if the absolute correctness of the diagnosis is of moment, beware of anticipation. Until the patient is prepared for it, the physician should sedulously forbear to intimate or broach things that may give his patient unrest, embarrassment or may violate his sense of decency. To many patients there is nothing more odious than the snatching away of covers, and the laying on of hands; it makes them stubborn and sulky, whereas, to patience and perseverance every necessary concession would be made. If a physician have an unusually delicate task to perform, let him in neither speech nor manner discover its extraordinariness, lest the patient, from the stress given the occasion, construe the necessary compliance into positive indecency. Bashful women—for the question can only be of women—would escape or refuse answer if time were given them to consider the magnitude of the seeming indecency. An unconditional, decisive question, put in a manner showing at once the necessity and the naturalness of the communication, will generally if not always evoke the desired answer.

To the patient's sense of shame, concession is to be made in so far only, as it is unprejudicial to a complete diagnosis. Everything that might make him fretful should scrupulously be obviated. The physician should spare his patient as much as is consistent with his duty; delicate and painful parts, for example, should neither be exposed nor handled too often. Heedless of this caution, the physician but too often gives the patient opportunity to interpret that lofty axiom that medicine knows not shame, in a most equivocal sense.

The physician should not content himself with an incomplete examination; neither should he extend it beyond all the bounds of propriety. In critical cases, the greatest acumen is called forth to perceive the indications from the several symptoms. In simulative and dissimulative cases, presenting an illusive and unfavorable prognosis, one may justifiably have recourse to innocent means to help make a diagnosis. Cases of doubtful diagnosis, the examination of which may be deferred, should be examined from time to time. Some cases admit but gradually of a diagnosis. Concessions may be made to the innocent humors of the patient, especially if admissions of value to the diagnosis are thereby made.

In his early practice the physician will often fail to make a diagnosis. Though he will almost always discover the symptoms of the disease and interpret them severally, yet he will often be unable to constitute them a diagnostic whole. This inability is directly due to inexpertness in diagnosticating; in part to an absence of typicalness in the disease; to symptoms insufficiently pronounced; and to the presence of incidental phenomena. The physician should never be precipitate in naming the disease; but rather aim to complete his diagnosis by repeated examinations. It is an error of the grossest kind, to hold that a diagnosis can be made by a mere sally of genius, or by resoluteness, venturesomeness, or guess-work of any description whatever. Hard study and close observation only will suffice to make a correct, a reliable diagnosis.

A fruitful source of defective, meagre and erroneous diagnosis, peculiar to the first years of practice, is forgetfulness to note *all* the signs and symptoms of the case, or to search for *all* evidences of disease. What young practitioner has not had his judgment misgive him, even after his best endeavors, that the diagnosis was still anything but certain;—has not in almost every case of his virgin practice remembered the omission of important points in the examination after having left his patient! To instance this thoroughly, let him, when next he has visited a patient, compare the symptoms as he has elicited them with the number necessarily or usually present in the disease, and he will find that his examination has been too limited, that he has forgotten to make some of the most necessary observations—not that he was unacquainted with them, but because the number of observations serially to be made was too large either to make or compare without introducing system. This seeming improvidence of memory is

clearly altogether due to a want of discipline
in examining. Here as in all other processes of
investigation, system only is reliable, and no amount
of finger-filleting or memory-assisting legerdemain
promises credible results. It must be evident that to
search for all signs and symptoms, diagnostic and supplementary, of a given disease; to elicit a score or two
of evidences, some method or rule must needs be
adhered to, if more or less that is important shall not
be forgotten or at the least risked of being forgotten.

Patients are often irritable, sullen, and headstrong,
owing to either natural disposition or disease. A
patient may be refractory owing, respectively, to
having already been subjected to unsuccessful treatment; having a physician not possessed of his confidence
forced upon him by importunate but well-meaning
friends; or he may be at variance with those about
him; finally, his forbearance from communication may
be attributable to reasons of a more delicate description. It will not be difficult to determine whether the
cause of this is to be looked for without or within the
patient; if without, it will often require much ingenuity
and tact to induce him to unveil a circumstance to the
hiding of which he is not altogether disinclined
to sacrifice the impending result of the disease. The
physician should prevail upon him by gentle and sin-
cere means; by creating hope; by removing everything that might give offense; by assurance of readily
desisting, on demand, from further treatment. This

is not, as it may seem on first view, a matter of little moment; for there is without question, nothing that renders the diagnosis more difficult and vexatious than a persistently stubborn behavior of the patient. And unless this peculiar antagonism can be reconciled to his purpose, the physician will do well to resign the case. Such a course will certainly be most justifiable, and no less in the interest of the patient than the physician.

The physician will, as a rule, if the disease is not of an immodest nature, communicate the result of his examination to the relatives or attendants of the patient; if, on the other hand, the disease is of an immodest or delicate description, he will confide it to the patient as subject to his discretion. Again, the nature of many diseases is not to be revealed to the patient of a sudden, but gradually; the nonsuspecting victim of incipient consumption should not be startlingly confronted with what is at best an almost inevitable death-warrant; and the highly nervous patient should not always be informed of the extent and gravity of his malady, at least not more than is necessary to secure compliance and co-operation. Other patients, again, are so torpid, so indifferent regarding the importance of their ailments, that they must needs be magnified to create the concern and solicitude necessary to successful treatment.

In the course of the treatment of tardy cases, the physician will often covertly be cross-examined by certain patients with reference to their complaint, its prognosis, etc. But he should, before unwittingly answering, give a rational interpretation to such questions, as "Doctor, What *is* your opinion of my case?" "You *know* that I cannot recover?" etc. The physician may, with few exceptions, take it as axiomatic that an unfavorable prognosis is never welcome; that such questions are almost always prompted by inquisitiveness, disinclination for further treatment, reluctance to incur further expense; or by the desire to evoke a bad prognosis, and thus have a pretext for changing doctors. Hence, the physician will regard most of these queries as so many disturbing incidents, which he must dispel or conciliate as best he can. It will often be found that the best interests of the patient demand expedients, not only to questions, that, nicely speaking, irreconcilably clash with the truth. In such straits, the physician should ever be mindful of the fact that the restoration of the patient to health is ever his chief aim, and that all his endeavors ought to be desiderative of this object. Again, whereas, every impression received by the patient, results, philosophically speaking, in either good or bad, therefor, every impression should be calculated with reference to its effect.

There is one adverse circumstance attendant on every sick person, against which the physician can not guard too closely, and which is more liable to rob him of his patient than death itself—namely, outside influences, or as it has aptly been termed, "Chatter-ing Hopes and Advices." Perhaps nothing in all medical practice, not even the death of the patient, is capable of giving the young practitioner such exquisite mortification, disappointment and thorough disgust for his profession, as the request to surrender his patient into more skillful hands, or what is, if possible, still more keen, his unceremonious dismissal. The young practitioner should well secure his patient's interests, as well as his own, against such unnecessary pesterment, by determinedly interdicting daily and hourly, if not all, communication of neighboring gossips with his patient, no matter what his disease! This is a point not at all, or at least not sufficiently, enforced in private practice. What patient seriously ill that has not a constant stream of visitors, and at all hours of the day! And how many such patients that are not literally visited to death!

The physician is almost daily consulted by patients whose cases do not so much demand medication as hygienic regulation. But, however simple, however little in need of any actual drug the case may be, the physician should never simply send the patient about his business with the jejune advice so much regarded as a mark of medical common sense: "That's nothing," "That will of itself disappear," "Your case requires no treatment," etc. Where the patient is intelligent and the case unmistakably simple, a few words of explanation and advice may indeed answer every purpose; but in the great majority of cases the patient wants to be "examined", and then nothing short of a ransacking of the whole person, and a complete detailing of the result will give satisfaction. Such a task will often require hours of time, but the young physician, in view of his abundant leisure, can well afford to undertake it, for besides acquiring facility and skill in physical and catechetical examination, the habit of laboriously and conscientiously examining will of itself beget a reputation for professional thoroughness and acquirements. But as it is at present, there is altogether too much sinecurism in the profession to secure the average patient a more painstaking interest than a look at the tongue and a feel of the pulse, in addition to the traditional quiz about sleep, appetite, and the bowels.

The physician should let no regards for pleasantness or convenience, deter him in any instance from performing those offensive but positive duties, though which in point of pleasantness do not rank above common scavenging. It is here where the young and the routine practitioner sin most; in shirking digital examinations of privities, and ocular inspection of excrements; in neglecting to make analyses, and in shunning all those disagreeables peculiar to the conscientious practice of medicine. The fastidiously genteel beginner is not altogether disinclined to employ another's finger, or to glove his own, for certain duties, fancied menial, and to make a large item in his bill for every violence done to his imagination.

' But let the physician beware of carrying his usefulness in the service of the patient too far. He should not permit himself, unless specially indicated, to be carried to such officiousness as to assist, in the presence of other help, in undressing the patient for the purpose of examination; in dressing him, moving him out of bed and back into bed; in arranging his bedding, and in making himself "generally useful." The profession, or at least many of its members, has, aside from this, suffered largely in public esteem from the assumption of offices, formerly exercised exclusively by a sort of professional menial. There is a practical as well as a metaphysical reason for avoiding such forward interposition of services. There is, namely, a certain conduct, confined to no caste, a certain letting one's self down, more easily felt than defined, which is inevitably sacrificial of dignity of character. In our profession we have but too many sorry and abiding illustrations of this fact.

It requires a peculiar talent to make passive a capricious, obstinate, struggling child. When the usual means do not suffice, recourse must be had to others. Though the physician will in unexceptional cases not allow the cries and struggles of the little patient to deter him from his purpose, yet in certain cases he will do well rather to conciliate this peculiar opposition than to provoke a fit of fright. The physician, in such circumstances, has the choice of making his diagnosis without the aid of the exploration; to wait until the paroxysm has subsided, or to depart and return some other time, with the hope of better success. Perhaps one of the most successful ways of dealing with these little unmanageables for the purpose of examining them, is to approach them in a well-darkened room, where they cannot distinguish the presence and manipulations of the physician from those of the attendants.

But, as has been said by a close observer of sick children, "There is a certain tact necessary for successfully investigating the diseases of children. If, when summoned to a sick child, you enter the room abruptly, and going at once to your patient, you begin to look closely at it, while at the same time you question the mother or nurse about its ailment in your ordinary pitch of voice, the child, to whom you are a perfect stranger, will be frightened, and will begin to cry; its pulse and respiration will be hurried, its face will grow flushed, and you will thus have lost the opportunity of acquainting yourself with its real condition in many respects. Besides this, the child once excited, will not subside so long as you are present. If you want to see its tongue, or auscultate its chest, its terrors will be renewed, and it will scream violently; you will leave the room little wiser than you entered it, and very likely fully convinced that it

is impossible to make out children's diseases." * *
* * "Your first object must be not to alarm it; if
you succeed in avoiding this danger, it will not be long
before you acquire its confidence. Do not, therefore,
on entering the room, go at once close up to the
child; but, sitting down sufficiently near to watch it,
and yet so far off as not to attract its attention, put a
few questions to its attendant. All your observations
must be made without staring the child in the face."

Children of one and a half to two years old will
already bear some rigor, but a doctor with the face of
an inquisitor will, as a rule, attain just the opposite of
his expectations. Children that have not yet the
power of speech, must first be made passive by tender,
affectionate treatment. If they indicate a part as
painful, the physician should assure himself that it is
actually the seat of pain; they often locate pain where
it is not. Half-grown girls should not be questioned
things they can not or ought not to know. For
information apply to the relatives. Girls, youths and
boys can often not be made to speak until those under
whose surveillance they are, absent themselves. One
should well mark their actions as well as their manner
of speech.

To become an eminently successful, or rather,
popular children's doctor, the physician must, at least,
be a putative if not a genuine lover of children. Not
that it is here contended for that a love for children
is, generally speaking, in itself absolutely requisite to

the proper management of their ailments, though in fine
it is, indeed, not unessential, but the doctor that is bar-
ren of all natural affection for children, and even too
remiss to hide his defect before the very eyes of the
fond parent, may be assured of being retired early
from this branch of practice. The doctor that comes
to the little patient with nothing in his countenance
that it may understand, that will question tartly in its
presence, that will summarily proceed to subject it to
an examination as unsparing of alarm to it, as it is
thorough; that will concede nothing in point of
omitting treatment and measures highly obnoxious to
it, will—no matter what his other professional abilities
—never be a favorite with the little ones, nor, as a
matter of course, with parents. It is an extensive fact
that popularity with the little patient almost always
outweighs medical competence in the estimation of
many parents. Thus the child insists on having the
sugar-plum doctor, and the indulgent parent, more than
gratified for an opportunity to do something accepta-
ble for the little darling, gladly consents. The sugar-
plum doctor comes, he speaks very softly, he smiles
sweetly, he is all obligation, he has his pockets filled
with good things, he is very indulgent, he never insists on wearying examinations or the examination of
parts not easily accessible, and, hence, never makes
his little patient fret or cry, nor does he prescribe
"nasty" medicines. And the sugar-plum doctor is
popular, or, what means the same thing in these pro-

saic times, he is successful. Without commending this for his imitation, let the young practitioner be advised so to conduct his management of this peculiar practice, that he may be of the most competent service to his little patients. But it is obvious that to be enabled to do so he must first possess himself of their patronage. Let him avoid extremes; let him not despise policy, but let his policy consist in honorable expedients.

ON PROGNOSIS.

"The practical test of a true science is the power which it confers of 'prevision,' or of knowing now what will follow hereafter. Some sciences have attained to this point, as we see daily illustrated by physics and chemistry; but as yet medical science has arrived at only very partial security of forecast. And yet the fore-knowledge of the consequences of a present disease, is that for which patients and their friends often seek from the physician with the greatest eagerness. When we can prognosticate with certainty, medicine will have become a 'science.' At present we only, with different degrees of nearness, approach this end. We may describe the 'probabilities' of a given disease; we may even measure them; we may accept or reject lives at insurance offices; or we may affix a numerical value to their duration; but we deal with doubts and not with certainties. Life is too subtle for us to know or measure all its possible contingencies; and our information is too scanty to render us thoroughly satisfactory interpreters of the outcome of any malady. But, with all this doubt, much may be accomplished for the safety of society, and the relief of individual anxiety or care."

The young physician should well mark that it is not

as is commonly believed and practiced, the province of the physician to predict the results, but only to estimate the tendencies of the disease. He should be mindful of the axiom that : "Inasmuch, as it is impossible to predict anything with certainty so long as we remain unacquainted with any one of the conditions of a given event, and ignorant how they may act in a particular instance; and, as in the living body, no occurrence or effect ever does take place constantly in the same manner at all times, we can never with perfect certainty predict any occurrence or effect whatever."

The physician should, as a rule, not state his opinion of the duration and termination of a disease, unless requested to do so, and then in a manner rather suggestive of the tendencies than the results of the disease. To attempt more than this, is to impose upon himself a task as hazardous to his reputation as it is unnecessary and foreign to his purpose, and the non-fulfillment of which is daily and hourly witnessed, in convalescence and decease, in change for the better and for the worse, notwithstanding all the prognostications to the contrary. Although the prognosis be correct, as in many cases it may, it is not always proper or advisable to make it known. For example, by a precipitate disclosure that the disease is lethal, and its course, therefore, inevitable, the physician will, at most, for his pains, procure his discharge, and an obnoxious course of treatment for his patient. In most cases, indeed, the physician may earn credit for himself and his profession by anticipating the course of events and communicating it.

Until the junior practitioner has acquired the forecasting skill of experience, his opinion of the tendency, duration and result of the disease should be based upon certain prognostic data, such as the deviation of the organism from health; the resistence of the constitution; the vitality of the diseased organ; and the degree of its involvement; the deviation of the disease from its acme; the suppression of the crises; the intensity of the disease; the amount of complication; the rapidity of the elimination of the diseased products; etc.

The principles that have been enjoined on the physician respecting the prognosis as a whole, should also be observed with reference to the particular disease and its various stages.   The educated physician will not prognosticate a definite number of days for the accession, culmination and resolution of a fever; nor will he on diagnosticating an incipient pneumonia, acquaint and terrify his patient with an inevitable stage of red and gray hepatization, or with possible cheesy degeneration.   The same may be urged for the measures probably to be employed.   Let him never be communicative about the remedies to which he may be obliged to have recourse; for every such confession surrenders up a certain amount of decisiveness, purpose and professional stability.

ON TREATMENT.

"In the prevention or treatment of disease our science culminates and becomes an art. Unless it can accomplish one or the other of these ends, the world would do as well without as with our aid. It is of some value to know the probabilities of our state, but it is of comparatively small value to have this knowledge if we can do nothing either to ward off, alleviate, or cure disease. We may prepare some people for the worst, we may dispel some groundless fears; but our mission is to do more than this: we have to try to 'cure the curable, and comfort the incurable.'"

In conducting his plan of treatment, the physician should not be too ready to condemn a remedy or measure if its efficacy is not immediately manifested. It is a fact of no inconsiderable moment, that the proper treatment is often sacrificed to impatient expectation. It is a very common and grave error to assume that the medicine has been administered or the treatment carried out for the reason that it was prescribed. The remedy may not have been taken, or, if taken, rejected by vomiting or otherwise eliminated from the system; it may have been insufficient or rendered inert; it may have been adulterated or inert. The prescriber or dispenser may have been

in fault, owing, respectively, to the prescribing of
chemical incompatibles, the mistaking of symbols,
carelessness, ignorance, dishonesty, oversight in compounding, misreading and miscopying of directions,
etc.   ·

Patients often have or develop an extreme aver-
sion for a medicine, owing to its continued exhibition,
its peculiarity, or to an idiosyncrasy of the patient.
Though the possible correction of this objectionable
particular is an old maxim of good practice, and
though the physician is by no means remiss in correct-
ing it when perceived, yet this species of surfeit is far
too often due to ignorance of elegant pharmacy in the
physician; and the patient's expressive: "I will not," or
"I cannot take that horrid stuff!" is but too often justified.   The young prescriber should, when inditing his
prescriptions, never be forgetful of what palatability
or rather, though it amounts to the same, insipidity,
has done for homeopathy.

Where the same medicine is to be exhibited for a
long time, some advertance should be had to tasteful-
ness.   Where the taste is necessarily (?) surprising,
extraordinary or very objectionable, the patient should
profidently be made acquainted with the reason for
the same.   As to idiosyncrasy, the pecularities of the
individual irrespective of temperament, it is a subject
altogether too much slighted in modern practice; the
physician seldom, if ever, adverting to it in his daily
routine.   Though experience is the only sure guide in

these cases, the physician should, where hazardous drugs and doses are to be employed, always question as to the presence of such constitutional peculiarities for either drug or dose. This will spare him much disagreeable experience and the frequent facing of the problem, why this person was not affected by more than a maximum dose, and that person almost poisoned by a dose less than minimum.

Where the right treatment for a given disease proves inefficacious after a reasonable trial, the integrity of the diagnosis, unless certain, should be question and redetermined. Where the diagnosis is certain and the treatment classic, yet inefficacious, the physician must individualize or the next most reputable remedy should be tried; if still without success, the association of counsel in the case, before entirely losing the confidence of patient and attendants, will be the most politic measure for the beginner whose reputation is still in the making. Where the diagnosis is quite certain, but the indication is not met by the treatment after a reasonable trial, the young doctor should for obvious reasons not follow the lax practice of the day—permit the repeated compounding of the same ineffectual remedy.

The physician should never, unless circumstances expressly call for it, familiarize the patient with the drugs employed by him. Neither should he ever enter into a parley with him respecting the merits of remedies, etc. To inform certain patients that it is quinine, potash, or calomel which is to save them, is to divest the remedy of its most potent charm— faith, and to surrender it to its repute with the patient or, what is the same, to his prejudices. Others, again, it is no less an error to leave altogether in ignorance as to the object of the remedy to be administered. Thus, for instance, the well-known feeling of indefinite expectation, or "moral effect," resulting in most persons on taking a dose of medicine, is, especially where the patient lacks confidence in the physician, almost always shaped by their preconceived notions of the medicine. This circumstance, this "moral effect" which is so frequently the only proper, the only curative measure available, is not sufficiently appreciated in routine practice, though in his diagnostic and therapeutic perplexities, the physician gladly. enough avails himself of it. What a subject for regret, that many daily cures, confidently attributed to some favorite remedy, cannot be shown to be due and due alone, as they are in fact, to this power!

The beginner in the practice of medicine cannot too forcibly be enjoined to adhere to the established canons of therapeutics, and not go in quest of new remedies. Here, as elsewhere in science, he should remember that no amount of vaunting and recommendation nor a score of isolated trials and favorable reports, suffice to give the stamp of proof to a reputed remedy. It will be a safe rule in this era of advertisement and multiplicative medicine, for the

beginner to discard every new reputed remedy, and
faithfully to follow the medical classics. He will
have neither the leisure nor the sanction of the patient's interests to discriminate the good from the bad*
in an infinitude of annual new-fangledness, nor to
venture experiments before having mastered the science of his profession as it is.

The physician should on coming in charge of a
case, in every instance inform himself of the reme-
dial means hitherto employed, domestic and other
remedies not excepted. This will, besides often spar-
ing him much useless drugging and valuable time,
better enable him to appreciate the present face of
the disease, where this has been more or less distorted
by therapeutic interference. The physician ought
always to acquaint himself with the diagnosis and
treatment of a brother practitioner, where he succeeds
him, by *regardfully* questioning the patient or attendants thereto; by *liberally* dealing with his measures;
and, where the case is peculiarly perplexing or where
it is otherwise demanded, by conscientiously reviewing his very prescriptions. Though the physician
can not respect the professional creed or competence
of a brother physician, and, therefore, not forego the
traditional smile and shrug of deprecation, etc., he
should at least regard the treatment, or interference
of his predecessor, as a fact, as an actual circumstance in the history of the case; and hence, though
not always essential to the diagnosis, almost invaria-

bly essential to a correct understanding of the case in its entirety.

Much of the success of treatment, no less than the frequent occurrence of vexing casualties in course of treatment, depends directly on the manner of giving directions to patients and attendants. The physician should make it a point in practice to give all of his directions at one time, and not scatter them over a half-hour's or an hour's conversation, or intersperse them with anecdotes and *bon mot*, which practice is quite sure to result in a family debate after his going, for the purpose of discussing and determining what all he has said and meant. The directions should be, it is at once needless and needful to say, exhaustive of the necessary nursing and other details, and leave nothing to be wished for in point of being explicit and expressive. Where the attendant does not seem to understand or is otherwise inapt— but too frequently the case—he should, as a matter of course, be instructed. Nothing gratifies an attendant or nurse more, especially an intelligent and experienced one, than precise and complete instructions, and nothing is as capable of so much prepossessing him in favor of the physician. There are many patients and attendants, chiefly young persons and the unsophisticated of the lower classes, who are so diffident or stand so much in awe of "the doctor" as to be afraid of asking the necessary information. Such self-insufficients should, provided the carrying out of the treatment is of any consequence at all, be made to repeat the directions after being plainly communicated to them. For it can not be gainsaid that the annoying mistakes and untoward accidents are altogether of too frequent occurrence, and prolific only from the sources animadverted on.

The physician should prescribe with a definite purpose and where there is a clear indication. This imports something more than is generally and usually apprehended under it: Making a correct diagnosis and finding the right remedy, which is by no means synonymous with good practice. The physician having made out the character of the disease, too often contents himself with being guided by the subsequent course of the "symptoms" and the product of the perfunctory quiz as to appetite, sleep, and bowels; whereas, nothing short of known pathological conditions, their extent and degree, together with their therapeutic correlatives, appropriate remedy and dose throughout the course of the disease, ought to satisfy him. On the whole, patients are not sufficiently often examined, and, therefore, the treatment not varied—adapted to the varying phases of the disease; they are too often misdrugged, too often under-dosed, and still more often over-dosed; the medicines too long and not long enough continued.

A source of much vexation and chagrin to the young physician, is to experience repeated prescriptions for the same ailment fail of making the slightest impression upon it. Such inefficacy of treatment is always tentative of shaking the correctness of the diagnosis and treatment, and, as a result, the confidence of the patient and his friends in the physician. On such occasions, having been disappointed after doing his best, and feeling the criticalness of his position, he anxiously casts about in mind for new and untried indicants and measures; not arriving at a definite result, and becoming more and more uncertain, believing, furthermore, that the patient or attendants are not altogether ignorant of his predicament, he instinctively begins to feel the necessity of making a more exhaustive examination, of finding a more appreciable idea of " what's the matter." But conscious of his short-coming, and fearful of exposing himself to reprehension or of losing his patient's confidence, he only partially re-examines and re interrogates. The result of some mechanical fumbling and desultory quizzing, not proving satisfactory, as might have been expected, he instinctively quits the subject of diagnosis for that of treatment. His mind now wanders, with much uncertainty and no definiteness of purpose, in quest of new remedies. Mentally rapidly reviewing the catalogue of materia medica, reverting to similar cases and their successful treatment, he finally seizes upon a remedy, though the plan of treatment is first shaped and matured after the books have been consulted. These brown-studies at the bedside are as needless as they are undesirable and profitless.

The result of every examination must invariably be a positive product, however insufficient for a complete diagnosis. Hence, the physician should at least know the *present* totality of the disease and be able to determine its *present* therapeutic affinity. However intractable the disease, however incomplete the diagnosis, the *present* facts can be the only measure for therapeutic effort. The corrective for an incomplete diagnosis and a persistent inefficacy of treatment must be looked for in supplementary examinations.

One of the most fatal quicksands to the professional success of the beginner, is, beyond question, the well-known class of incurables, whose purpose of existence would seem best explained by their predilection for young, because painstaking practitioners, and by their peculiar fitness for damaging reputation. There is hardly another source of more frequent disparagement to the profession and of humiliation and chagrin to the physician than those chronic wrecks, who, Banquo-like, haunt the profession, who have done all but died and been buried, and who, having made the rounds of all materia medica and therapeutics or the entire surgical armamentary, finally issue from the gantlet of the profession as, in public estimation, martyrs to medical bungling. In view of the fact that it is quite impossible to cure most, or at least many, of these cases, the young physician should, whatever difficulties and tasks he may be willing to encounter in the consciousness of his ability, advisedly avoid by all manner of means this class of cases to whom disease has, as it were, become a normal condition, and who have successfully defied the best efforts of a score of good practitioners. Let him not begin his practice by staking his reputation, though yet a blank, against what is at best a mere possibility of a prize. Let him ween himself fortunate if the halcyon days of his sinecurism remain undisturbed by these forlorn hopes. But if he can not well avoid taking such a case, then let him be careful to impress the mind of his patient with the necessity for the requisite time to effect a cure. Let him verbally stipulate a term that will suffice for thoroughly mastering the case and employing the various resources for it. Let him, furthermore, if the case promise to prove incurable, and he has endeavored his best, associate reputable counsel with himself, that the brunt of the unreasonable blame inevitably following may fall upon one who is better able than himself to carry it.

Another fact, that the young prescriber doubtlessly knows but does not appreciatively enough act upon, is that, to the successful treatment of children's diseases, the palatability of his medicines and the unobjectionableness of his measures to the patient, are at least as important as the correctness of the diagnosis itself. For what does it avail him to have made a correct diagnosis, if his medicines are not administered or his measures carried out! And that the fond mother refuses, again and again, to provoke a struggle with her darling to administer what she herself admits to be at best but a disgusting potion, is a matter of daily observation. The physician's dismissal from the charge of a case is to be attributed at least as often to the prescription of measures and medicines repugnant to the child, and therefore to the parent, as to mis-diagnosis and positive mistreatment. What more suggestive hint of the proof of this fact does the physician need than the old, old story that the child refuses to take its medicine! And, else why is it that homeopathy is so popular, so " successful," with certain classes, especially in children's diseases, if it is not by reason of the absence of taste in medicine that is supposed to be present! Let the young practitioner canvass the merits of homeopathy in the estimation of its patrons, and he will find that all assertion and commendation of its " superiority over allopathy and other systems " resolves itself, besides its shibboleth " success," into the one great prestige " the medicines (!) are so nice to take." Or is the popularity of homeopathy with its patrons perhaps due to their being so very familiar with the philosophy of the doctrine of S. S. C., that they are in fine convinced of its truth! Though homeopathy, judged from a psychological point of view, is but a species of *system in insanity*, yet, like many other errors of the mind, it has been of incalculable benefit to the healing art, as revealing what nature, aided by judicious nursing only, can effect. Let the young therapeutist never be forgetful of this fact.

There is one branch of his art in which the graduate is so lamentably deficient, and about which he is as ignorant when he leaves college as when he entered it. This is dietetics—not with reference to his own needs, but to those of his patients. No educated physician will now question the great import of dietetics in the treatment of disease, and yet the young physician knows almost next to nothing about it. It is not necessary that he should be able to boil, roast, bake and broil to know something of dietary, but he ought at least to have a knowledge of its principles. Perhaps the largest field for successful treatment is offered in diseases of the stomach. But so long as there prevails the astounding spectacle of the same dyspeptic patient making the rounds of a dozen doctors, and being informed by them successively to eat everything; to eat nothing; to take solids only; to take fluids only; to eat much; to eat little, etc., so long specialists only will work this field successfully.

FROM GRADUATION TO PRACTICE.*

The graduate in medicine beginning the practice of his profession directly after receiving his diploma finds himself in a position not unlike that of many a newly arrived traveler in foreign parts at his first essays to speak and understand the language of the country. The chances are that the traveler's sole knowledge of the tongue has been acquired in a limited series of "lessons" at home. With his own master he thought himself tolerably proficient, but abroad the inhabitants seem to talk the language in a different way, they have other voices; their expressions are peculiar; they make strange gestures; and utter their words so rapidly. The result is that, while the bewildered stranger catches here and there a familiar word or simple phrase, his diagnosis of the general meaning of what is said is apt to be very vague and confused.

The plight of the embryo practitioner is not much better. His mind is stored with excellent medical precepts, together with a fine assortment of correct prescriptions. He can discourse to his patient right learnedly, but, alas! like our traveler he can talk better than he can understand. In his mental outfit are the keys to diagnoses of numberless diseases, but for the particular case in hand none of them ever seem to fit. The cases which the young practitioner meets all appear to be anomalous ones. He recognizes as familiar certain features, certain symptoms, but then there are other symptoms that are certainly out of place and incongruous. The art of medical observation, the art of appreciating symptoms at their proper value, has not yet been acquired. The tyro is unduly concerned about "pathognomonic " symptoms, and is very prone to hasty generalizations— in a word, lacks practical experience. His three years' "curriculum " has afforded him more instruction than training, and it is only the combination of these two elements, that makes a complete education. The training of practical observation and experience is necessary before his knowledge can profit him. Knowledge is power only when conjoined with wisdom. The studies of the medical student are so crowded with matters new and strange to him, they embrace subjects of such a varied character and so infinite in number, that the mind can afford but little activity to any faculty save that of memory. He emerges from the course with a vast collection of facts, but with very little individual judgment. His judgments are those of his professors; he scarcely dare make his prescriptions original, and his diagnoses are sure only when he meets the counterparts of cases he has been shown at the clinics. Alma Mater sets her young brood adrift to complete its evolution alone. She dubs the graduate "teacher of medicine," when yet he has the most to learn. Is it safe to trust this fledgling alone? He has his feathers, and much he may plume himself on them, but little he knows how they are to be used; he has yet to be taught to fly. The element of training is still lacking in his education. How is this to be obtained?

Without further instruction, the young graduate may adopt the independent course of beginning practice at once, trusting to time to remedy his defects. The objections to this course are that the experience, besides being acquired very slowly, is often warped by early prejudices that result from too partial observation, and impaired by careless methods of practice that are liable to become confirmed habits. The paucity of the material observed leads often to conclusions that a wider field and more friction with other observers would have shown plainly to be erroneous. Many succeed well in spite of these drawbacks; and, though it may be said of these practitioners, as of other self-made men, "It is better to be self-made than not made at all," it is none the less the duty of the physician to avail himself of every facility at his command to make his equipment for the intelligent practice of his art as thorough and complete as possible.

When the recent graduate has the opportunity of forming an association with an established physician of large practice, where his work is under the controlling influence of an older and more experienced head, his advantages are increased, but such an arrangement has also its disadvantages. The control, which at first serves as a valuable check and guidance becomes in time a great hindrance to independence of opinion. The habit of referring every question to his superior checks the evolution of his own judgment, and tends to render him a mere reflection of the opinions of one man. Moreover, these opinions are not likely to be uniformly enlightened on all subjects. Every physician of position and experience has his strong points, but upon others his authority is less reliable. Indeed, few are free from more or less faulty prejudices. It is, perhaps, especially important that the young physician who assumes the relation of assistant or junior partner to an older practitioner should already have formed a broad mental groundwork of sound, catholic opinions.

With regard to the uses of the dispensary system in our large cities, there is much to criticize. The material afforded for study is vast and of incalculable value, but, unfortunately, the manner in which it is generally used is most wasteful, and in too large a degree profitless. A young physician, often entirely inexperienced, is placed in charge of a class, averaging from, say, ten to fifty or more new patients a day. There is a certain consciousness of official dignity in disposing of so many cases within the allotted hour. His patients are from an inferior class, that he looks upon with unavoidable disdain, and regards as simply so much food for science—and, were this food digested as it should be, more good would result both to science and to the patient. As it is, the material is bolted as rapidly as possible, occasionally pausing for a "snap" diagnosis of an "interesting case," but with little appreciation of the advantages that are being squandered. While the conscience of the attending physician can ordinarily be trusted to deal in tolerably good faith with the patients he sees, he has neither time nor usually sufficient incentive to make such careful investigations as should be made. The physician is too isolated, too irresponsible, and slip-shod work is too much the rule. The average dispensary class by no means affords that sort of training to the young graduate which he especially needs.

In a large hospital the system is vastly better. The "House" acts as the teacher of his assistants, and his work in turn is under the supervision of the attending physician. The members of the staff are in intimate association with one another, and their intercourse affords friction which keeps up enthusiasm in the work and tends to raise its standard. The experience gained by the *interne* of such a hospital is unexcelled by any method of medical training. But it has its limits. The term of service is a short one, and, though the cases observed embrace a wide range of diseases, there are many classes of affections which are rarely met with except in certain special institutions. Moreover, the conditions of the service often confine the *interne* to a certain department of the hospital, where he is exclusively concerned with a particular set of diseases. The arrangement is doubtless a wise one, and is attended with good results, so far as thoroughness in the work is concerned, but it nevertheless leaves the young physician at the end of his term of service still but partially prepared for all the exigencies of a general practice. The training he has received enables him to acquire what remains with comparative ease. In a good measure he has acquired the scientific habit, the art of weighing evidence as evinced by symptoms, the habit of recording observations, and, moreover, considerable expertness in making a diagnosis. His mental receptivity is also greatly increased. He can better digest new facts and estimate the value of new methods and theories. It is at this period that the medical novitiate has generally, where practicable, sought the advantages of foreign instruction.

Until recently there has been little or no provision in this country for the pursuit of such studies as are demanded at this period of the medical education. Abroad, at hospitals and polyclinics were courses especially designed for the practitioner—courses of short duration, several of which could be pursued together, and in which the matriculant was brought in contact with an abundance of classified material which he was enabled to study under the guidance of experienced specialists. The necessity of seeking these

advantages abroad is, fortunately for the great majority'of young physicians, becoming every year less. In
the past few years much has been done to supply the
requirements of practical clinical instruction which
recent graduates demand. A number of classes in
various special departments have been established in
different institutions, and have uniformly been well
attended. The two schools which have been opened
in this city within the last few months, with the especial
object of supplying the demand referred to, demon-
strated the fact at once that such a demand was
urgent. There is reason to believe that, in the future,
schools of this character will form an important acces-
sory of medical education. The plan of instruction
that before had been followed in special institutions
has in these schools been systematized and made more
comprehensive. Many who seek instruction have
already seen something of practice, and what they require is not didactic teaching, but practical demonstra-
tion. They wish to see exemplified upon patients the
proper methods of diagnosis and treatment by those
whom long and special study has qualified to speak
with a degree of authority.

Such are the facilities afforded the medical graduate to perfect his training for the practice of his profession. A word with regard to his *animus*—to the
motives which should actuate him in this preparatory
work. Unfortunately, in the pursuit of our profession,
there are two important motives which are liable to

conflict. One is scientific, the other commercial. But there need be no conflict; the two motives should be made coincident. For the practitioner an undue prominence of either is a loss. The physician wholly engrossed in the scientific aspects of his profession will have indifferent success as a practitioner. He may gain κῦδος, but few shekels. The doctor who practices with an eye single to his fee is false to his oath and false to his patients. In the early studies of the young physician, the commercial spirit is especially noxious. It belittles his professional aims and lowers the standard of his preparatory work. The desire for prosperity is a legitimate incentive, so long as it does not predominate. The greater the interest in his work, the more likely that it will be effective and fruitful. But the prevailing motive should be the desire to acquire competence in his art; all else should be subordinate. A competence in his pocket will follow, and it will be seen how commercial aims may coincide with the legitimate requirements of science. But interest of some kind he must have that is live and active. The spirit that actuates him must be a thoroughly earnest one, or little will be accomplished. The most productive work is always that which is directed to ends in which the mind takes an absorbing interest. This interest in the medical man may be greatly augmented by judicious attention to his natural predilections in the choice of particular departments of study.

After the elementary or fundamental part of his medical education is completed, the physician soon finds his natural tastes and aptitudes tending spontaneously toward certain special lines of medical investigation. By properly heeding these intimations he will not only add a spark of enthusiasm to his study, but, by giving his work a more definite direction, he will improve its quality. The attempt to cover the whole field of medicine uniformly will only result in superficiality. The aim should be, while striving to to acquire proficiency in all departments, to attain excellence in one. The best work in medicine, without doubt, is being done in the "specialties." The specialist has a peculiar enthusiam in his adopted department of study, and, moreover, the minuter his study the wider the field that expands before him, and the more it impels him onward. The farther he goes the better he appreciates the fact that the *consensus* of all the medical sciences is such that to excel in one branch of medicine he must also be proficient in all its sister branches. There are *artisans* in special medicine to whom the term "mere specialists" justly applies, but the specialist has no true title to the name who is not also a good physician.

It is not, however, the writer's intention to advise every young doctor to become a specialist. What he would urge is that each choose, sooner or later, some particular line of study in which he shall aim at an especially high standard of excellence, and from which, as a good point of departure, he can better attack the whole field. A wall intervenes between him and success.   It is wiser first to effect a breach at some one point than to attempt to batter it all down at once.   The fowler who singles out a particular bird in a flock will be surer of his game than he who makes a random shot at all. It is not designed that other departments of study shall be neglected, but that at some point there shall be a glow in his work; and the fire of enthusiasm once kindled will soon inflame the whole.

THE MATERIAL OUTFIT.*

With all the natural acumen a man may possess, and with all the education he may have fortified himself with, there are certain material appliances without which it is vain to attempt the practice of medicine at the present day. No one man needs them all; some need more of them, some fewer. In general terms, these appliances may be divided into instruments, materials for dressings, and more or less of a stock of medicines.

Of all of them, he whose lot is cast in the country will require more at the outset than his city *confrère*, for the latter, being near the sources of supply, may forego the acquisition of the greater number until he actually has occasion to employ them, whereas the country practitioner must be *nunquam non paratus*. There can be no question, however, but that both are apt to imagine at the start that it is well to provide themselves with an array of instruments, and the like, most of which will never be of any more use to them than the show-bottles in an apothecary's window.

Discretion comes into play very decidedly in the selection of such appliances as the physician needs to have in his possession. There are certain articles of

every-day use that cannot be omitted, of course—the
thermometer, the hypodermic syringe, the pocket-case
of minor instruments, a spirit-lamp, a specific-gravity
bulb, a few test-tubes, and the more ordinary reagents
for testing urine. These must be had; the question
is, how to select them. The first piece of advice we
have to give is, do not buy articles that are cheap.
Nothing is sold much below the ordinary price unless
there is some factor in the case that will afterward
account for the low price, to the disgust of the pur-
chaser. It would be well for the graduate to buy the
necessary outfit before leaving the city in which he
has pursued his college course, and it will be of advantage if he can get some older practitioner's advice
in its selection. If he happens to have taken his degree at a country college, it would be better to write
to some acquaintance in the city, rather than corre-
spond directly with the dealer, for the latter, with the
best intentions possible, is quite likely to misunder-
stand his customer's wishes. Much disappointment
would often be saved by paying a physician for the
trouble of making the selection.

As a general thing, it is not well to invest in novelties. Often an instrument that seems extremely
well adapted for the purpose it is intended to serve
will turn out to be of little or no practical use. Appliances made of soft rubber had better not be
obtained until they are really wanted for use, as that
material is apt to deteriorate rapidly.

In regard to medicines, it is mostly the country practitioner that needs to keep them on hand, but even him we should advise not to invest heavily in them, unless the field of his practice is quite remote from an apothecary's.

In the matter of drugs, too, it is well to avoid novelties, except under unusual circumstances. We would repeat, also, what we took occasion to remark in regard to instruments, that it is poor economy to buy cheap articles. They are always dear at any price.

THE HOSPITAL COURSE.*

No man can be said to have prepared himself properly for a creditable career in medicine unless he adds some practical training, under competent supervision, to the learning he has acquired in the college course. Rarely will any other form of such training be found fully to take the place of a term of service on the house staff of a general hospital. We would, therefore, beyond all things else, urge the young graduate to leave no stone unturned to secure such a service. Even an opportunity to form a business connection with an established practitioner should not be allowed to stand in the way, for any man who is judged worthy of such an association at a time when he has barely emerged from the medical college, is most assuredly the very one whom a hospital course will most develop, and to a certainty he is the very one who can afford to give up the glittering bauble of the present, and rely with well-grounded confidence on the incomparable advantage that such a training will bring him in the course of a few months. Too many men suffer all other considerations to be overshadowed by the reflection that they have spent a good deal of time and money in acquiring the right to practice, and by the consequent conviction that they ought to begin earning a living as soon as possible. This is a grave error. In the long run, nothing is gained by beginning to practice at an early age; one will achieve competence quite as soon by starting upon his actual work at the age of thirty as by setting out at the age of twenty-five. Time is not lost, therefore, but put out at interest, so to speak, by devoting it to the completion of one's education. We do not mean to say by any means that the hospital course is absolutely essential to success in practice, for we are quite aware that our profession includes many men of deserved eminence who in their early years were compelled to forego the great advantage it confers; but we do say, and that without the slightest hesitation, that, of two men equally well prepared in other respects, he who has seen hospital service will tread a path comparatively smooth, while the other will have to wage a wearying warfare with the deficiencies that it is the precise result of such service to do away with.

What is the charm by virtue of which the hospital course does all this for a man? The fact that it gives him the best "graded course" possible, under the guidance of the best practitioners with whom he could by any means be thrown. We will state, in general terms, what it is. Having passed his hospital examination, the young man enters upon the duties of a Junior Assistant, Junior "Walker." If his service is on the medical side of the house, but little is generally required of him in this grade: he makes the daily rounds with the House Physician, and again with the Attending Physician; drinking in *savoir faire* from both; when not thus engaged, he superintends the details of medication, especially of external applications, applies cups, leeches, and the like, passes the catheter, and does such other minor manipulations as may be thought a little too much for the nurse and rather beneath the dignity of the Senior; he also copies the latter's histories of cases into the record books. ' For the time being, he is a "general utility man;" but the familiarity with details he thus picks up is wonderful, and he really comes to be very "knowing." Become a Senior, his leading duty is to elicit and note down the patients' histories, and on occasions he figures as "House" pro tem. When he actually becomes "House," he bears the immediate responsibility in the management of the cases; aided only by the Attending Physician's daily visit, he has the entire direction of the treatment. He thus .acquires confidence that never deserts him. On the surgical side the gradation is much the same, *mutatis mutandis.*

It will be seen that by degrees the young man advances from a position of no responsibility to speak of, to one demanding and begetting the utmost self-reliance. In most, if not all, of our hospitals in New York, the candidate for a position on the house staff of a hospital must first have passed his examination for the doctorate; in some cities, as we understand, this is not the case. It seems to us that the former system is by all odds the better one; it insures that all the medical officers of the hospital shall be "qualified" practitioners, and it allows the young men to devote all their energy to the actual work before them, unhampered by the perfunctory systematic study of books that an impending examination really obliges them to undertake.

Something is to be said in regard to the choice between various hospitals. In the first place, we would advise a general rather than a special hospital. It need not be a large one, for too large a service requires so much sheer work in its performance that thoroughness of observation is apt to be neglected. The field afforded by a special hospital is of great value, no doubt, but, if possible, a course should be taken in an institution where the practice includes the whole range of medicine and surgery. Least of all would we advise the young graduate to take a position in a lunatic asylum, but, for that matter, there is not much likelihood of his being able to get one. Psychiatrics is so very special in its scope that it does little toward preparing a man for general practice; and, on the other hand, good service can scarcely be rendered in a lunatic asylum by those who have not had considerable training in a wider field.

We can not close without a word to those modest men, who hastily conclude that a hospital career is beyond their reach. They cannot all attain to it, to be sure, for hospitals are few; but any man who is fit for such an appointment can usually secure it in the end. Some of our best men have failed at the first trial, and afterward been rewarded with success. Above all, let our readers free themselves from the fear of favoritism. With very few exceptions, our hospitals are open to the best men, no matter whence they come or where they got their degree. At any rate, it is no disgrace to fail in the attempt, and they often succeed who enter the contest with but faint hope.

THE OPPORTUNITIES FOR THE STUDY OF MEDICINE IN NEW YORK CITY AFTER GRADUATION.*

In my opinion, the best opportunities for the continuation of the study of medicine, after graduation, are to be found in hospitals. A large hospital is better than a small one, for the young practitioner should, if possible, see a large number of cases, and become rapidly saturated, as it were, with experience.

When private practice is entered upon, there will usually be ample time for the careful and deliberate study of a few cases. The number of large hospitals is, however, limited, even in New York. Besides, to enter one, the graduate must pass an examination, one that is competitive and usually much severer than that which gave him his degree.

But a few months as a resident in a small hospital afford a larger experience, and give more opportunities for practical work, than does time spent in any other way. Making a rude estimate, it may be said that there are from one hundred to one hundred and fifty places of all kinds, in hospitals large and small, general and special, that are to be filled annually in New York. When we remember that from four to five hundred men are graduated every spring in our city, we see that, at best, only about one man in four can get a place. I fear, however, that some of these places go a begging in our city, although those in Bellevue, New-York, Roosevelt, Charity, St. Luke's, and a few others, are eagerly sought after. Indeed, great and special preparation is made for passing the difficult examinations that are a prerequisite to getting one of these places. The young men who cannot get these desirable places should by no means abandon the idea of securing a hospital position. The position of a clinical assistant or dresser, and finally of a House Physician or House Surgeon, in one of the smallest hospitals in New-York, is, in my opinion, better able to prepare a man for active general practice than even a lucrative place as an assistant or junior partner to a very busy medical man.

Senior partners are usually too busy to give much attention to instructing their associates, and it is just where the senior has become rusty that the young doctor, fresh from a college, needs to fix and assimilate his knowledge. The attending surgeons and physicians of hospitals are usually on frank and cordial terms with the house staff. They have none of the stiffness that they may assume as college professors, and he must be a very dull scholar who does not get very valuable notes on the cases in the wards from these gentlemen.

When the young doctor has assimilated the knowledge he has obtained in a college by a hospital course, he then appreciates the intuitive skill of a busy practitioner. He can then learn, by looking on, while in turn his own resources add something to the joint stock of knowledge and experience. But if the recent graduate has already been in a hospital, or if, from one circumstance or another, he cannot enter one as a member of the house staff, what can he do? Still I say, come to New York, or stay in New York. If you have a decent stock of preparatory knowledge, a great deal of industry, good health, indomitable will, and about four hundred dollars in cash, or available funds, you will be a much better prepared general practitioner in six months than the average of those whom I have known after they have been five years in the profession without post-graduate training. A list of all the medical facilities of New York —one comprising the colleges, undergraduate and post-graduate, dispensaries, hospitals, general and special—should first be made. You will find all this in the New York "Medical Register," although not compactly arranged. Then, at the most, three or four subjects should be selected, to which three or six months may be devoted. Suppose, for example, general medicine, diseases of the skin, and gynæcology are selected. In these departments you may have a weekly clinical lecture by such men as Flint, Delafield, Loomis, and Leaming, by paying the matriculation fee at their colleges. Then, for twenty dollars, you may have private instruction at the Polyclinic or Post-Graduate School, with visits to the hospital or dispensary with your private instructor. In skin diseases you may get Socratic, practical instruction by Sturgis, Bulkley, Fox, and others. ,In gynæcology, Dawson and Mundé will give you instruction in private classes, as a part of their post-graduate courses, while you may go to the weekly clinics at the undergraduate colleges, held by Thomas, Polk and Lusk.

From Addis Emmet may be had an occasional opportunity to see operations at the Woman's Hospital, on presentation of your card. Thus I might go on. Diseases of the throat and nose, of the eye and ear—all have their hospitals, to which the recent graduate is welcome, if he will hang up his hat and sit down, and not saunter about as if he were some distinguished visitor who has just dropped in for a half-hour. Private courses in the ophthalmoscope, the laryngoscope, otoscope, and microscope, are given in connection with the post-graduate and under-graduate schools and at the hospitals, at hours and times that can be readily ascertained, and for fees that are very small. At many of the dispensaries and hospitals the attending surgeons are always short-handed for clinical clerks and assistants. A man who will attend regularly for some two or three weeks, so as to get ac-

quainted with the staff, and who will attach himself
to one physician or surgeon, will soon find himself
well appreciated, and actually installed as an assistant,
without examination, with unlimited opportunities for
studying and observing the effect of treatment upon
diseases. If post mortem examinations be what is
desired, at Bellevue rare opportunities are given,
while Satterthwaite, Peabody, and others, give private instruction in normal and pathological anatomy.
The dissecting rooms of the colleges are also open to
graduates, during the winter and spring, on payment
of the fees. In a month or so of regular visiting to
the hospitals, a hard-working and modest man will
make acquaintances in his particular department of
study, who will give him an occasional opportunity
to see private operations, and to go to the various so-
cieties, public and private, and to hear the discus-
sions. If the recent graduate has but a few weeks,
the post-graduate school and polyclinic will furnish
all the opportunities he can use. If, however, he has
months, these will not furnish all he can enjoy and
profit by. The time has come, in our country, when
even country villages and hamlets are critical as to
the quality of their medical advice. A young man
who has lounged about a physician's office for two or
three summers, and spent but two short winter ses-
sions at a medical college in a large city, will stand
no chance by the side of one who has given three
solid years to the earnest study of his profession in

the college, and then added to that a number of
months of practical work, where his responsibility is
shared by an older head. The mere degree of M.
D. has, fortunately, come to have slight significance.
The medical schools of New York are becoming
more and more accessible. When I say schools, I
mean not only those strictly so called, but the hospitals and dispensaries, as well as the colleges. Di-
rectors and governors realize their responsibilities in
the direction of opening them to students. Every
year it becomes easier to get instruction. I would
earnestly advise any recent graduate, no matter what
branches of our science and art he wishes particu-
larly to cultivate, to stop in New York before he goes
to London, Paris, Berlin, or Vienna. .From some experience in all these cities, I think New York now
offers to the English-speaking student advantages
quite equal to those to be obtained in the old world.
If, after graduation, a man can stay a year or two in
hard work in New York, and then go abroad for a
few additional months, he will, to my mind, have ideal
opportunities. But better is it to stay here after
graduation, if the two kinds of post-graduate instruction, that at home and that abroad, can not be obtained.
There are master minds here as well as in the old
world.

POST-GRADUATE STUDY IN EUROPE.*

In advising a person who has just graduated at a school of medicine as to what would be the best course for him to pursue in a trip to Europe for the purpose of continuing his studies, what we have to say depends entirely upon the length of time which he intends to remain abroad. If there is no hurry, and two or three years can be taken for it, there are points which would be of the greatest value to know.

First of all, as to the expense. Germany is a cheap country to live in, and is also, I think, by far the best one to learn medicine in. It ought not to cost more than from forty to fifty dollars a month, with everything included. I know of a young man who lived in quite an expensive place in Germany, viz., Heidelberg, for twenty-five dollars a month for three years.

But before getting to Germany, and, in fact, before leaving this side, it is decidedly advisable to go to some respectable broker, and have all the money you carry changed into English money, since this is at a premium all over Europe, and anyone is glad to take it, whereas it is often not the case with other money.

Now as to the method of getting there. We all

have our own ideas about transatlantic travel; but, after we have landed, one thing is well worth consideration. In England and on the Continent never take a first-class railroad ticket, for the second-class one gives you just as much comfort in traveling, and costs just two-thirds as much as the first. It is an old saying in Germany that no one ever travels first-class except princes, green Americans and fools.

Of course, in order to get as much out of a trip to the old country as possible, it is necessary that we should know the language of the people among whom we expect to reside. And, since Germany is by far the best place to study medicine in, we must either be already acquinted with the German language, or we must acquire a certain familiarity with it as soon as possible, and, in order to acquire this, there are many things to be observed. First of all, it must be firmly resolved not to speak any more English than is absolutely necessary; therefore, when once in Germany, avoid all American and English people, as they will certainly keep you from learning German.

Again, it is desirable to take lessons in German; but be particular to select a teacher who does not speak English; *and on all occasions speak German, whether you make mistakes or not.* It is really remarkable the facility with which the inhabitants learn to understand a foreigner when he tries to tell them something in their own language, even if he does not use a single word correctly. The theatre is also a fine place to get the ear accustomed to the sounds of the words, and especially since on the stage they speak the best German, and pronounce it most distinctly.

If one has some time to spend abroad, by all means he should go to some *small university town* like Heidelberg or Würzburg, Jena or Giessen, and start with *histology* and *pathology*, since in these places there are not so many novel things to distract, and also the professors and their assistants will devote more time to a single person; they are all more or less fond of Americans, especially if they find them to be diligent. As soon as they see that you wish to learn, they will go to any length to teach you. I remember that, when in Heidelberg, I had looked but a few times through a microscope, and could hardly tell an air-bubble from a red blood corpuscle. Professor Arnold, the pathologist, was quite amused at first, but would sometimes sit for two hours by my side, and pour pathology into me as if with a spoon.

Spend the whole morning in the laboratory of pathology, for there you can also learn histology; after dinner, in the laboratory of physiology, and you will certainly be surprised at the amount of science you will absorb and the rapidity with which you will learn the language.

I had a friend who went to Jena and avoided all Americans for one year, then came to Heidelberg and passed his examination, obtaining the first degree in his Ph. D. in one year and a half. This I remark only to show how the language can be learned by avoiding all English-speaking people, throwing off false modesty, and speaking German continually, whether you make mistakes or not, as before observed. It would be well after the first semester (term) to attend the lectures and some of the clinics, but never miss a post mortem when it can be helped, for they make them in a different way from what we do generally.

After a year and a half or two years, you may go to a larger town, and the selection will depend upon the special branch which you are desirous of paying attention to. Vienna is the best for obstetrics, diseases of women and children, and skin diseases, and also possibly for ophthalmology and otology, but for the latter branches Heidelberg is very fine. Moos, for the ear, is the very best man, since he does not have many students, and will devote the whole time to one man if necessary. Becker has the finest eye clinic in Europe, and is also very kind to students.

For surgery, Berlin, Vienna, or Munich is the best, but the last not so good as the others.

For pathology, no one is so renowned as Virchow in Berlin, but for this branch all of the universities are good. For microscopical pathology, the same may be said about the universities, but the preference might be given to Würzburg, Heidelberg, and Strassburg.

It is far more difficult to advise anyone who only

intends to spend six months or one year in Eurôpe, but, nevertheless, as a general rule, what has been said about a longer period may be applied here also, with the exception that it will be almost impossible, in so short a time, to acquire enough of the language to understand a lecture or appreciate the fine points that any teacher may make. In this case I would spend at least half of the time, say six months (if one year is at disposal), in the laboratories of *pathology* above all, and then in those of physiology.

About these there can also be said a good deal which may be useful. For instance, if a person understands the language he has a great advantage, but if he does not, then I think he should select some place where he can use English, as in Heidelberg.

Professor J. Arnold, who directs the laboratory of pathology, speaks English quite well, and is perfectly willing to speak it. His assistant, also, Professor Thoma, speaks English very fluently, and is fond of speaking it. So here is a rare chance.

Also in the laboratory of physiology is Professor Kühne, who speaks English, French and German almost with the same fluency. Again, his assistant, Professor Ewald, has as good a command of our language as we ever find in a foreigner. Therefore, when there is only a year, Heidelberg is certainly the place in which to spend six months of it. There is another point to be considered, viz.: if it be possible, let this be in the spring and summer, for during those seasons it is one of the most beautiful places on earth, but the winter makes it very disagreeable.

After a time has been spent with the microscope in a smaller town, of course it is then advisable to go to the largest clinics to be had, where as much as possible can be seen. For this Berlin and Vienna are the places, but the latter has the preference over the former for many reasons. Then, also, it will be winter, and that part of Europe is then much pleasanter than the latitude of Berlin. If you intend to spend the winter in Vienna, you may go directly from Heidelberg to Switzerland for the midsummer, when the universities are closed, and be near your winter home without loss of time or money.

If anyone is already more familiar with French than he is with German, and desires to acquaint himself with the French school of medicine rather than the German, he may go to France. In this case it would also be best to spend the first part of his time in one of the smaller towns. France, however, is not like Germany in having such a multitude of smaller places of learning; but as for the larger cities, we all know there is but one—Paris. In that city the hospital advantages are the finest, and much time could be advantageously spent there. I am, however, inclined to think that the teaching in France is not quite so systematic and thorough as in Germany, since they are more apt to indulge in "glittering generalities," than to confine themselves to pure and absolute science. However, as a happy mean, where we find all the plodding perseverance of the German system, and the fascinations of the French character, we may select Strassburg; where we find both a French and a German population, and may learn both the languages at the same time. But neither Strassburg German nor Strassburg French is of the purest. A word about Great Britain. As to hospital advantages, there is no city in the world where they are greater than in London, but the same objections hold good for the teaching in England that we have found in the case of France. Pathology, however, can be studied to the greatest advantage in Edinburgh, whereas, for physiology, no place can be better than the laboratory of Professor Foster in Cambridge. The English surgeons are very brilliant, as we all know, and we may devote much time, if we wish, in England to the branches of surgery and physiology, and also much to pathology in Scotland.

The particular advantages of the larger cities we may say are: *Vienna*, obstetrics, diseases of women and children, surgery, skin diseases, ophthalmology, otology, and hospital practice; *Berlin*, pathology, surgery, chemistry, physiology, ophthalmology, and hospital practice; *Paris*, surgery, physiology, ophthalmology, and hospital practice; *London*, surgery and hospital practice; *Cambridge*, physiology; and *Edinburgh*, surgery and pathology.

---

*The articles marked with an aste isk (*) are taken from the New York Medical Journal, with the kind permission of the editor.

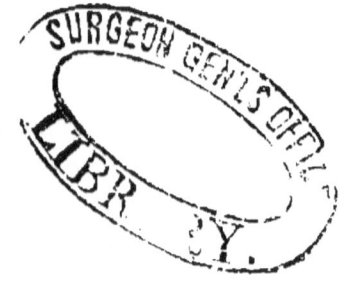

THE STUDENT'S MANUAL OF HISTOLOGY.

By CHARLES H. STOWELL, M. D., Professor of Physiology and Histology, and Instructor in the Physiological Laboratory, University of Michigan. Second Edition. A much needed text book for the student of Histology, and a complete guide for the practitioner and microscopist. Illustrated with 192 wood engravings. Cloth, price $2.00.

THE UNTOWARD EFFECTS OF DRUGS.

A Pharmacological and Clinical Manual, by DR. L. LEWIN, Docent of Materia Medica, Hygiene and Public Health, in the University of Berlin. Second Edition, revised and enlarged. Translated by J. J. MULHERON, M. D., Professor of Principles of Medicine, Materia Medica and Therapeutics in the Michigan College of Medicine, Detroit, Michigan. It discusses the accidents and effects of drugs which are frequently very embarrassing and liable to be confounded with symptoms of the disease. Price, $2.00.

THE BUSY PHYSICIAN'S VISITING LIST.

Pocket Ledger and Clinical Aid. The advantages of this list are its perpetuity, its contents of chapters on Differential Diagnosis, How to meet Emergencies, A List of New Remedies, A Blank Clinical Record, A Blank Record of Births and Deaths, A Monthly Summary of Practice, Table of Pulse-Rate at Various Ages, Obstetric Calendars, Cash and Expense Account, Metric Tables, etc. It is strongly bound in best Russia leather. Price, $2.00.

NITRO-GLYCERINE as a Remedy in ANGINA PECTORIS.

By WILLIAM MURRELL, M. D., M. R. C. P., Lecturer on Materia Medica and Therapeutics at the Westminster (England) Hospital, etc. This work gives directions for the administration of Nitro-Glycerine as a remedy for Angina Pectoris. Price, $1.25.

WHAT TO DO IN CASES OF POISONING.

By WILLIAM MURRELL, M. D., M. R. C. P., Lecturer on Materia Medica and Therapeutics at the Westminster Hospital, Assistant Physician to the Royal Hospital for Diseases of the Chest, London, Eng. A handsome little pocket manual in cloth, gold embossed. 95 pages. Price, 60 cents.

— 3 —

HOMŒOPATHY.—WHAT IS IT?

By A. B. PALMER, M. D., LL. D., Professor of Pathology and Practice of Medicine in the College of Medicine and Surgery in the University of Michigan. SECOND EDITION—An able exposition of the fallacies of the Homœopathic system. Cloth, price $1.25.

NEW THERAPEUTICAL AGENTS.

By WILLARD H. MORSE, M. D., Pittsfield, Mass. This little work gives intimate knowledge of the recent additions to the materia medica from a therapeutic point of view. Two hundred pages. Price, $2.00.

ORGANIC MATERIA MEDICA.

By L. E. SAYRE, PH. G., of Philadelphia. A conspectus of organic materia medica and pharmacal botany. A valuable work. Cloth, price $2.00.

THE HAIR: ITS DISEASES AND TREATMENT.

By C. HENRI LEONARD, A. M., M. D., Professor of Medical and Surgical Diseases of Women, Michigan College of Medicine. Octavo 320 pages, beautifully bound in cloth; 110 illustrations. Price, $2.00.

REFERENCE AND DOSE BOOK.

By the same author. This book contains the doses of more remedies than any Dose Book published. Besides this, full tables of antidotes to poisons, urinary tests, and many pages of miscellaneous matter are given. Cloth, 16 mo., pages 100; post-paid, 75 cents.

GOUT IN ITS PROTEAN ASPECTS.

By J. MILNER FOTHERGILL. M. D., M. R. C. P., London. This is a practical treatise on a subject comparatively little understood in this country where the grosser manifestations of the disease are rarer than in England. Price (8vo., 300 p.), cloth bound, $2.50.

DIPHTHERIA, Therapeutic Gazette Investigation of.

This book of 120 pages contains the replies of upwards of a hundred representative physicians, to questions touching the etiology, path-

ology and therapeutics of diphtheria. These replies are also summarized, and the conclusions to which they lead are concisely stated.
Price, in paper, 75 cents; in cloth, $1.00; in boards, $1.25.

Any of the above will be sent, postage prepaid, on receipt of price.

Address,

GEORGE S. DAVIS,

P. O. Box 470.   DETROIT, MICH.

www.ingramcontent.com/pod-product-compliance
Lightning Source LLC
Chambersburg PA
CBHW020807020726
47495CB00008B/2621